DANGER at the BREAKER

by Catherine A. Welch
illustrations by Andrea Shine

Carolrhoda Books, Inc. / Minneapolis

To my husband and children — C.A.W.

To the two Emmetts in my life — my son and his dad — A.S.

Text copyright © 1992 by Catherine A. Welch
Illustrations copyright © 1992 by Andrea Shine

This book is available in two editions:
Library binding by Carolrhoda Books, Inc.,
    a division of Lerner Publishing Group
Soft cover by First Avenue Editions,
    an imprint of Lerner Publishing Group
241 First Avenue North
Minneapolis, MN 55401 U.S.A.

Website address: www.lernerbooks.com

Library of Congress Cataloging-in-Publication Data

Welch, Catherine A.
    Danger at the Breaker / by Catherine A. Welch ; illustrations by
    Andrea Shine.
        p.   cm. — (Carolrhoda on my own book)
    Summary: Because of family need, an eight-year-old coal miner's
    son in 1885 leaves school to work at the mines, where he learns
    about the dangers of a coal mine on his first day on the job.
    ISBN: 0–87614–693–0 (lib. bdg. : alk. paper)
    ISBN: 0–87614–564–0 (pbk. : alk. paper)
    [1. Coal mines and mining — Fiction.] I. Shine, Andrea, ill.
    II. Title. III. Series.
    PZ7.W4486Dan 1992   91–16514

Manufactured in the United States of America
2 3 4 5 6 7 – JR – 08 07 06 05 04 03

Author's Note

Life in the coal mining towns of northeastern Pennsylvania during the 1800s was not easy. The mines were dark, rat-infested, filthy, often wet, and dangerous. Men worked 10 to 11 hours a day bent over in the tunnels, breathing harmful gases and coal dust. Many died in accidents. Fires, cave-ins, floods, and explosions were common.

Many mining towns were run by the coal companies. The companies provided poor housing and often cheated the miners of their full wages. Families were forced to shop at the company store and pay its high prices. As a result, some women had to take jobs in factories to earn extra money.

Women also had the difficult task of keeping the house clean. Homes in the coal towns were covered with coal dust, and water was scarce. Most people did not have running water in their houses. So women spent many hours hauling water for washing clothes, cleaning, and bathing. During the hot summer months, a separate shed behind the house was often used for cooking and bathing.

At the breaker—a building outside the mine—coal was crushed, washed, and sorted according to size. Boys under the age of 16, some as young as 8 or 9, worked in the picking room. They breathed the unhealthy coal dust while sorting out the useless pieces of rock. They worked 10 to 11 hour shifts, 6 days a week, for as little as 45 cents a day.

Some boys worked in the mines as doorboys. They sat alone in the dark, waiting to let carts, carrying coal and miners, through doors that connected the underground passages. The doorboys opened and shut these doors, which controlled the flow of air within the mine. If the doors were not shut quickly, deadly gases could build up and explode. Everyone's safety depended on the boys doing their job correctly.

The coal mining families all suffered the same hardships. But they were from many different ethnic and religious backgrounds. Instead of helping each other, they quarreled and often made things worse. But they did pull together when disaster — such as a mine accident or a house fire — struck. Then, everyone helped. And there were times when the people put aside their differences to enjoy a weekend baseball game or summer picnic. After many years, they finally learned that the only way to better their working and living conditions was to join together.

Danger at the Breaker is a fictional story about a special day in the life of a coal miner's son — the day he starts working as a breaker boy.

Andrew sneaked along the side
of the rickety cooking shed
and pressed his ear to its rotting door.
He could hear his parents talking inside.
"I sold more berries
to the company store," said his mother.
"A few more quarts, and Andrew will have
some new school clothes."

"Andrew won't be going to school
anymore," said his father.
"The boss says there's a place for him
as a breaker boy."
Andrew's mother slammed a kettle
onto the coal stove.
"But Andrew's too young!" she shouted.
"He's only eight years old."

"I know," said Andrew's father.

"You're right. He is too young.

He'll be the youngest boy at the breaker.

But the boss says

there's a place for him *now*.

And we need the money.

I'm sorry. But I'm going to tell Andrew

that he starts tomorrow."

The talking stopped.

The floorboards creaked.

Someone was coming to the door.

Andrew jumped behind a bush.

The door flew open,

and his mother ran out crying.

Andrew watched her stumble

barefoot over the stones.

We do need the money, he thought.

But will I like being a breaker boy?

That night, Andrew had trouble sleeping.
He thought his father's job must be awful.
His father always came home
with a rattling cough
and covered with coal dust.
His mother had to scrub
his father's aching back every night.

Andrew thought back
to what his father had said.
"He'll be the youngest boy at the breaker."
None of Andrew's friends
had started working at the breaker.
He wouldn't know anyone there.
And he wouldn't know what to do.
These thoughts kept Andrew
tossing and turning.

The next morning came too soon.
It was still dark
when Andrew was awakened
by the cry of the breaker whistle.
He slipped into his clothes
and gulped down some oatmeal.
Then it was time to leave.

Andrew and his father walked silently
along the misty footpath.
When they reached the work area,
Andrew's father pointed
to a tall, crooked building
outside the mine.
"That's the breaker," he said.
"That's where you'll be working."
Andrew saw the building.
He also saw the breaker boys.
They were playing football.
"You go on over," said his father.
"I'll see you later."
Andrew watched his father walk away.
He watched until his father
disappeared underground
with his pick and shovel.

Then suddenly—whack!

Andrew felt a slap on his back.

"My name's Patrick,"

said a husky voice.

Andrew spun around.

"Patrick Kelley, that is,"

said a boy twice Andrew's size.

A dozen boys were following Patrick.

They circled around Andrew.

Andrew looked down at his feet.

The ground was a thick mat
of coal dust.

Patrick leaned closer to Andrew.

"I've been here the longest,"
he told Andrew.

"I know everything about the mines."

Andrew glanced at Patrick's hands.

They were covered with cuts and bruises.

Patrick stared Andrew
straight in the eyes.
"You know, they make you go down
into the mine tunnels
if you work too slow."
Andrew squirmed
and dug his feet into the coal dust.
"You ever been down in the tunnels?"
Patrick asked, prodding Andrew
with a football.
Andrew shook his head.
"You won't like it.
They take you down a thousand feet.
It's as dark as night.
And as still as death.
The only sounds
are the crumbling rocks
and rats running in the trickling water."

"And if the rats don't get you,
the tunnel might cave in,"
said another boy.
"There could be an explosion!
The gases could snuff you out.
A mine tunnel could flood.
You could drown."
Just then, Patrick nudged the boy.
"Pipe down. The boss is coming."

The chattering stopped.
An angry-looking man
marched toward them.
"Patrick Kelley," barked the man.
"You're doorboy today.
Get over to the mines."
Patrick's face turned white.
He stumbled off
as if he were wearing lead shoes.

"The rest of you follow me,"
shouted the boss.
Andrew followed with the others.
Before they entered the breaker,
the boss turned to Andrew.
"You Andrew Pulaski?" he asked.
"Y-y-ess, sir," Andrew stammered.

"You'll work next to Brian," said the boss.
He grabbed one of the boys by the sleeve.
"He'll show you how to pick slate."
Andrew looked at Brian.
Brian was taller than Andrew,
but not much older.
Andrew thought he seemed friendly.
Brian smiled at Andrew
and nudged him into the building.

Inside, the breaker trembled and roared
with the rumble of machines.
The room was like a big cave,
with everything blackened by coal dust.
Brian led Andrew under a catwalk
to a wooden bench next to a chute.
"Sit here and watch me," he shouted.
Just then, a roll of thunder
rumbled at the top of the room.
Andrew looked up.
A load of coal tumbled down a chute
and traveled along a moving belt.
Andrew watched
as rollers crushed the chunks
and hurled the pieces past screens.
The pieces were washed with water,
then fell through holes in the metal sheets.

Finally, a stream of coal
tumbled down the chute
in front of the boys.
Brian stooped over the chute
and swiftly snatched out
some bits and pieces.
"Let the shiny coal chunks pass by,"
he told Andrew.
"Pick out the scraps and dull bits.
Then toss them into that box next to you."

Andrew nodded and copied Brian.

Coal clattered down the chute.

Andrew reached forward.

He searched for the useless pieces.

Another stream of coal rushed by,

scraping his hands.

Andrew quickly pulled out the rocks.

He tossed them into the box,

then stopped to look at his hands.

His knuckles were bleeding.

"Get goin'," shouted Brian.
"The boss is watching!"
Andrew glanced up
at the platform above them.
The picker boss loomed overhead
like a watchdog.
Andrew nervously reached into the chute.
His fingers scrambled to keep up.
"Don't ever take your eyes off your work,"
warned Brian.
"Or you *could* lose a finger."

Lose a finger!
Andrew shuddered at the thought.
Quickly he fished out the rocks
from the stream of churning chunks.
He didn't dare look up or stop.
He didn't want to lose a finger.
And he didn't want to be sent
to the tunnels for working too slowly.

The morning seemed endless.
The clatter of coal
and the screeching of machines
made Andrew's body shake.
The cloud of gray coal dust
stung his eyes.
His nose was clogged.
His fingers were stiff.
His back ached from hunching over.
I wish I were back in school,
thought Andrew,
back with my friends.
I'll never like coming here every day.

Hours later, the whistle blew.

It was noon.

Time for their lunch break.

For Andrew, lunch was a chunk of bread
spread with jam.

It wasn't much.

But after the long morning,
it would taste good.

Andrew and Brian talked
as they left their places
with lunch pails in hand.

"Don't believe everything
Patrick tells you," said Brian.
"They won't send you into the mines
for working too slowly.
But watch out for the picker boss.
He looks to see
if you're picking out all of the rocks.
If you're not, he'll kick you
or hit you with a stick.
Sometimes he'll even crack your knees
with a hammer."

Suddenly—

BOOM! BOOM! BOOM!

An explosion shook the area.

Wh-e-e-e-w! Wh-e-e-e-w!

The breaker whistle howled.

Everyone raced out of the building.

Andrew didn't move.

He didn't know what to do.

Brian grabbed his arm.

"Come on," he cried.

Outside, men scrambled in all directions.

Workers raced to the site,

carrying stretchers.

Miners stumbled out of the mine,

coughing and gasping for breath.

A horse, hauling a cartload of coal,

limped behind the men,

then collapsed.

The breaker boys huddled together.
They watched and waited.
A few more men
came staggering out of the mine.
Patrick was among them.
He was covered with dirt.
"What happened?" Brian shouted
over the blaring whistle.

"I opened the door
for the coal cars to go through,"
said Patrick.
"All of a sudden,
there was an explosion."
Patrick gasped
and stumbled to the ground.
"I'm never goin' back there again."
Two of the boys helped Patrick.
Andrew and Brian crept closer to the mine.

Andrew looked for his father.

He could not find him.

What if Dad's trapped? thought Andrew.

He could be crushed. He could drown.

He could be gassed to death.

Andrew felt his head spinning

and his knees shaking.

He slid to the ground.

By now, miners' wives
were rushing into the area.
Some were clutching babies.
Some were dragging children by the hand.
Andrew's mother was one of the women.
Andrew's heart beat faster.
He pulled himself up
and ran toward his mother.
"Dad is still in there," he cried.

Just then, Brian spotted a miner
being carried out on a stretcher.
Brian raced toward him.
Andrew and his mother followed.
The man was Brian's father.
His face was cut, and his clothes were torn.
"My husband," cried Andrew's mother.
"Pulaski—did you see him?"

Brian's father shook his head.
"He was in the tunnel below me.
After the blast,
the timbers crashed down,
and part of the roof caved in.
He never came out."

Andrew and his mother waited.
Deep in the tunnels,
workers labored with picks and shovels
to free the miners.
Time was against the trapped men.
Soon, they would be without air.
But working carelessly or too quickly
might cause another cave-in.
The hours passed.
It was getting dark.
No one came out of the mine.
The whistle was silent.
The hustle and bustle
outside the mine had stopped.
Andrew thought back
to what Patrick had said—
"still as death."

Finally, a few miners
limped weakly out of the mine.
Andrew stood up.
He looked at the first man.
It was not his father.
Andrew looked at the second man.
It was not his father.
Three more men followed.
None of them were his father.
Andrew felt a gentle hand
on his shoulder.
"It's time to go home,"
said his mother.

Slowly, Andrew and his mother
walked away.
They did not speak.
When they got home,
Andrew's mother went to the shed
to prepare a bath for him.

Andrew sat by the front window.

It was too dark to see much.

But Andrew kept staring and hoping.

After a while, his mother called out,

"Bath's ready."

Andrew was about to turn from the window.

But wait, he thought.

I think I see something.

Andrew searched the darkness.

There was something out there.

Andrew could see a dim light.

A man was coming up the footpath.

The man was wearing a miner's hat.
Could it be Dad? Andrew wondered.
The light glowed more brightly
as the man came closer.
"Daddy's coming," Andrew shouted.
"Daddy's coming!"

The next day,
Andrew returned to the mines
with his father.
And for many years,
Andrew worked as a breaker boy.
He never forgot
what happened that first day.
He never got used to the noise,
the dust, or the threat of danger.
But it was something he had to do.
Because that was life
for a miner's son,
many years ago.